T0145288

To order additional copies of this book, contact:
Xlibris
844-714-8691
www.Xlibris.com
Orders@Xlibris.com

ISBN: 978-1-6698-1890-8 (sc)
ISBN: 978-1-6698-1889-2 (e)

Print information available on the last page

Rev. date: 03/31/2022

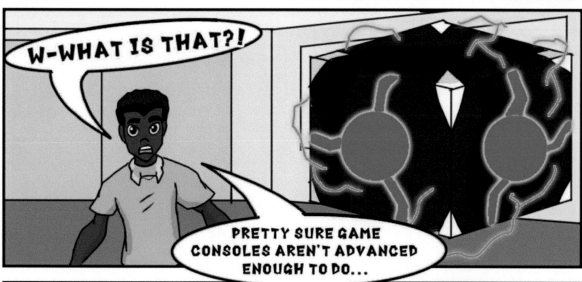

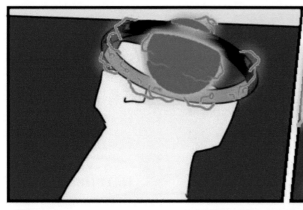
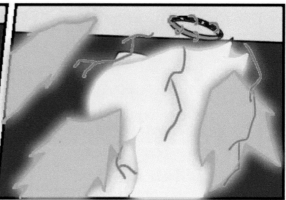

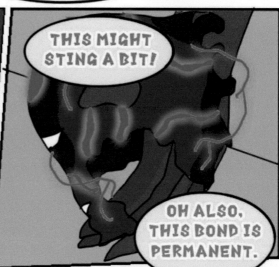

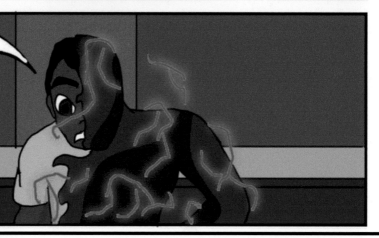

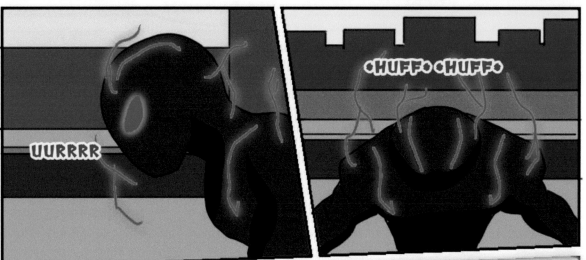

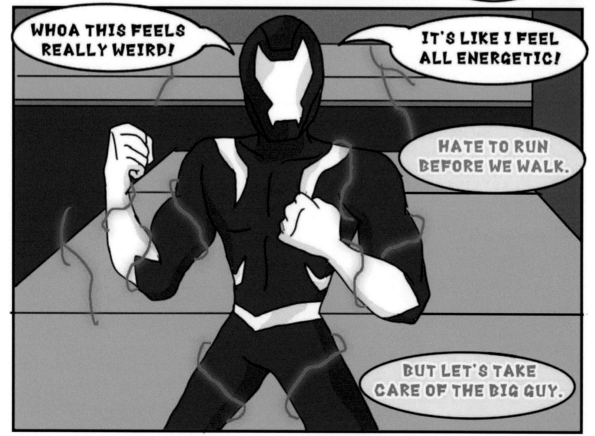

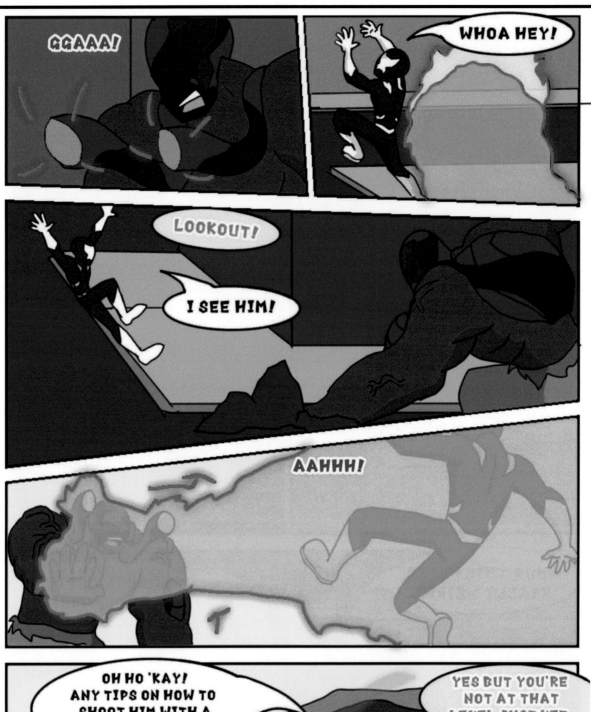
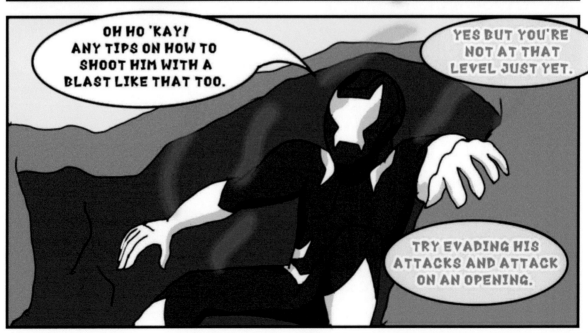

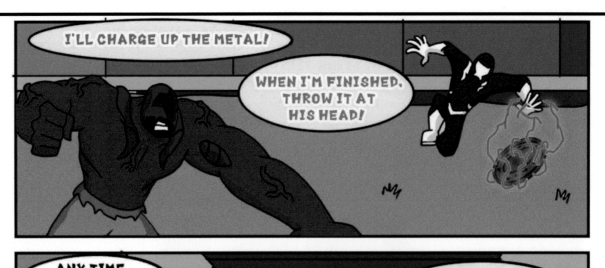

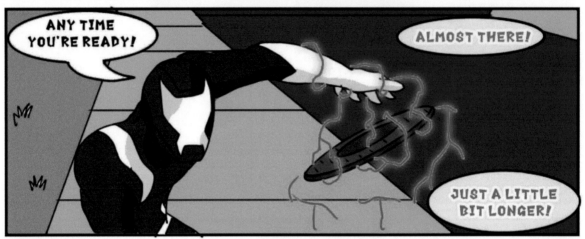

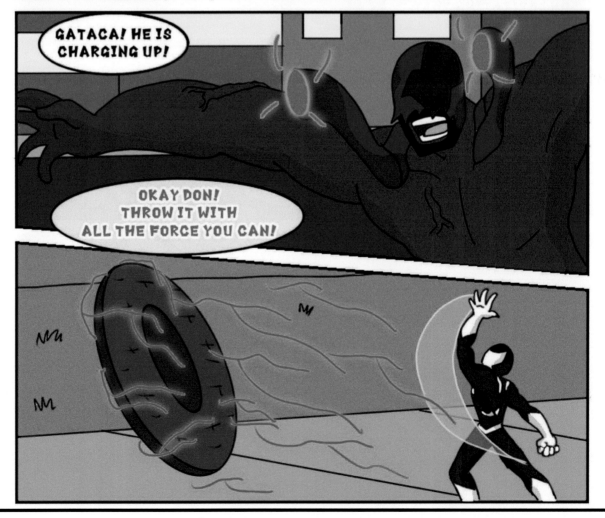

ISSUE #2

T.E.N
TELEPATHIC.EXTRATERRESTRIAL.NANITES

NEXT ISSUE : " TRAINING BEGINS"

CREATED
WRITTEN AND
ILLUSTRATED BY
DEION TILLETT